Mad About

Chicks, lambs, and other

farm animals

make
believe
ideas

Hens and chicks

Hens are female **chickens**. They have layers of soft feathers that keep both the hens and their **eggs** snug and warm.

comb

chick

Rooster

Male chickens are called **roosters**. They can wake up everyone on the farm with their early morning cry, "**cock-a-doodle-doo**!"

rooster

hatching

Cock-a-doodle-doo!

rooster

Mad about hens

The world's largest hen's egg was laid in China. It was just over 3.5 in (9 cm) long.

Hens can fly, but not very far. Getting over a fence or into a tree is usually their limit!

Chicks will hatch out of their eggs after about 21 days.

Hen eggs are usually white or brown, but they can be green, blue, or even pink!

ear

horn

beard

Goats and kids

Goats are smart animals that
are curious about everything.
A **nanny** or a **doe** is a female
goat. A male goat is called a **ram**
and a baby goat is called a **kid**.

Mad about goats

The world's longest goat horns were 52 in (132 cm) long—that's over six times as tall as this page!

Some goats can jump up to 5 ft (1.5 m) and some can even climb trees.

Both male and female goats grow beards! These are the tufts of hair under their chins.

Some goats give milk, which can be made into butter and cheese.

horns

ram

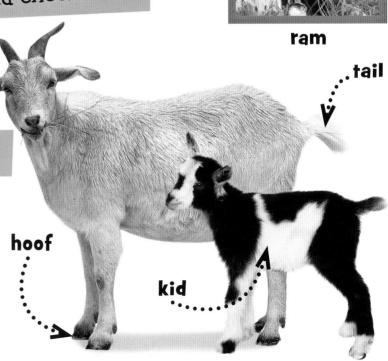

tail

hoof

kid

Fussy eaters

Although **goats** nibble on most things, they are actually very **fussy** and only eat the best quality food!

Ducks and ducklings

Ducks like to splash about in rivers, streams, and ponds. They stay **waterproof** by spreading a special **oil** over their feathers.

beak

duckling

Super swimmers

Using their **webbed feet**, ducks can **swim** in really cold water because their feet do not feel the cold!

webbed feet

Mad about ducks

Ducks were named for the way they dip (or duck) underwater to find food.

Some ducks can fly as far as 332 miles (534 kilometers) a day.

Ducks make their nests using feathers plucked from their chest.

In 2008, a charity raced a record-breaking 250,000 plastic ducks along a river in London, England!

Mallard duck

feather

Geese and goslings

wing feathers

Geese are large waterbirds that can live in and out of **water**. A group of geese is called a **gaggle**.

Mad about geese

Geese like to eat slugs, snails, and even mice!

The largest Canadian geese have a wingspan of 6.5 ft (2 m), which is twice the size of a child's arm span.

Baby geese are called goslings.

Geese are not friendly to visitors, so they can make good guard dogs!

Canadian goose

goslings

wing feathers

Flying

True geese **migrate**, or travel, from northern areas, where they have their **young**, to southern areas that are warm for the winter. Farm geese do not migrate.

Farmyard fun!

Use your stickers to make
a farmyard scene!

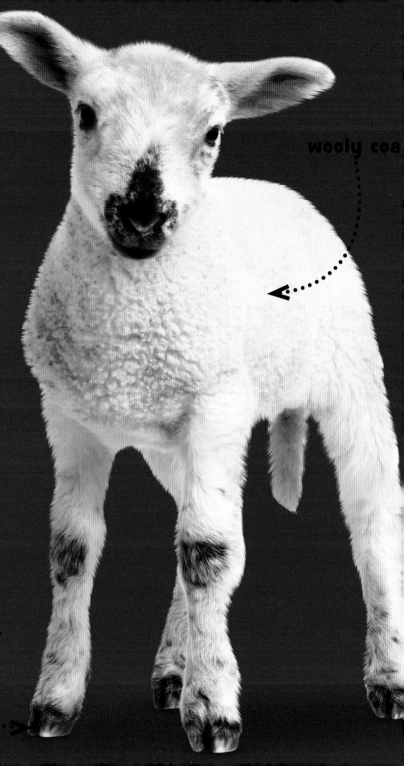

Sheep and lambs

wooly coa

Sheep are grazing animals, which means that they feed on grass. **Lambs** are baby sheep, which grow up to be **ewes** if they are female and **rams** if they are male.

hoof

Mad about sheep

Sheep can smell things through their feet!

In Australia, there are more sheep than people!

A sheep's wooly fleece is greasy, so that the rain will run off it.

One sheep's fleece will make about three wooly sweaters.

flock of sheep

ram

Warm and wooly

Sheep grow a wooly coat, or **fleece**, to keep warm in cold weather. Farmers cut off the fleece and use it for **wool**.

fleece

Cows and calves

Cows are raised in groups called **herds**. Female cows are kept for their **milk** and are called **dairy** cows. Male cows are called **bulls** and can be kept for breeding.

cow

calf

Mad about cows

Cows can chew on their food for up to eight hours a day!

A cow's stomach is divided into four special sections to help it digest its food.

The oldest cow ever was called Big Bertha. She lived to be 49 years old and had 39 calves!

Cows produce around 5.2 gallons (20 liters) of milk a day—that's about 80 glasses.

bull

calf

Beautiful bangs

Highland cows are originally from Scotland in the United Kingdom. Their long **bangs** help protect their eyes from disease.

Horses and foals

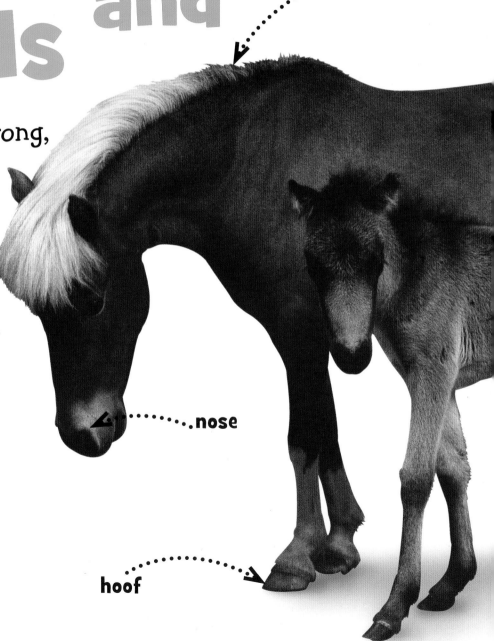

mane

Horses are strong, hardworking animals. On the farm, they can help the farmer pull **plows** and **carts**. A baby horse is called a **foal**.

nose

hoof

Horseshoes

Horseshoes are glued or nailed to a horse's **hoof** to protect its **feet**. It might sound painful, but it doesn't hurt when a horseshoe is put on.

horseshoe

tail

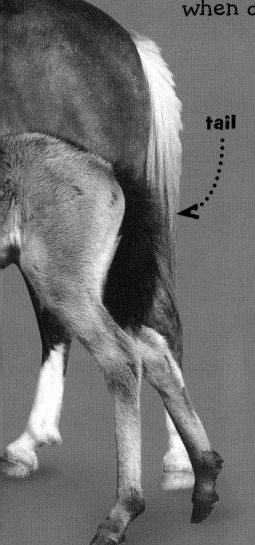

Mad about horses

Horses can sleep standing up!

Because a horse's eyes are on the side of its head, it can see two ways at once!

Horses are measured in "hands." One hand is the same as 4 in (10 cm).

The world's smallest horse is called Thumbelina. She is 17 in (43 cm) tall, which is only twice the height of a cat!

Pigs and piglets

With a **curly tail** and snuffling snout, pigs are easy to pick out! A mother pig is called a **sow** and a baby pig is called a **piglet**.

tail

piglet

snout

Mad about pigs

Pigs are very smart. They can be trained like dogs and are sometimes kept as pets!

Pigs have four toes on each foot but they only walk on two of them—so they look like they are trotting on tip toe!

Pigs have an amazing sense of smell and are used to sniff out special mushrooms called truffles.

piglet

pot-bellied pig

Muddy pigs

In hot weather, **pigs** love rolling around in the **mud** because it keeps them cool! It also gives them protection from the sun.

muddy leg

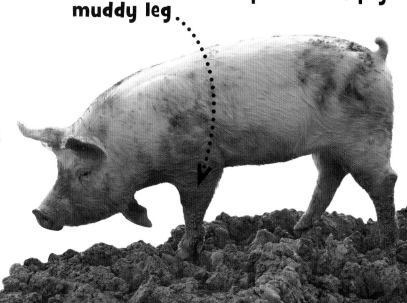

Guess who?

Look at the pictures, read the clues, and guess the farm animals!

1  I have webbed feet. I make a nest using my chest feathers.

2  I feed on grass and I grow a wooly fleece to keep warm.

3  I have long hair that covers my eyes. It protects them from disease.

4  I wear special shoes on my hooves. They protect my feet.

5  I grow a beard of tufty hair under my chin. I also grow horns.

6  I am small and fluffy. I usually hatch out of my egg after 21 days.

Answers: 1.Duck; 2.Sheep; 3.Highland cow; 4.Horse; 5.Goat; 6.Chick.